This book is dedicated to the
Earl and Countess of Carnarvon
with thanks for bringing
Finse into our world.

Love Finse

THIS BOOK
BELONGS TO

_____

_____

"Finse's First Journey"

The right of Karine Hagen to be identified as the author
and Suzy-Jane Tanner to be identified as the illustrator
of this work has been asserted by them in accordance
with the Copyright Designs and Patents Act 1988.

First published by Viking Cruises 2013. Reprinted 2016
83 Wimbledon Park Side, London, SW19 5LP

ISBN 978-1-909968-00-4

www.finse.me

Produced by Colophon Digital Projects Ltd,
Old Isleworth, TW7 6RJ, United Kingdom
Printed in China.

FINSE'S
FIRST JOURNEY

Karine Hagen
Suzy-Jane Tanner

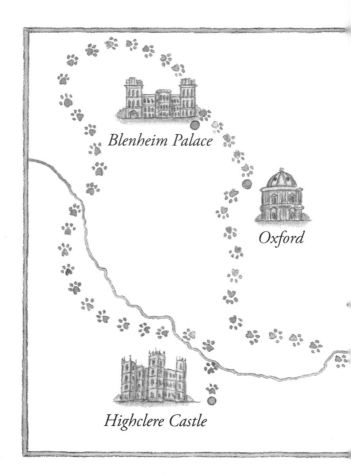

Blenheim Palace

Oxford

Highclere Castle

FINSE'S
FIRST
JOURNEY

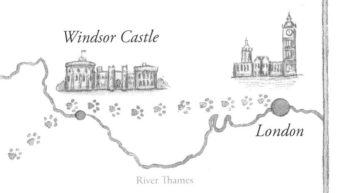

Windsor Castle

London

River Thames

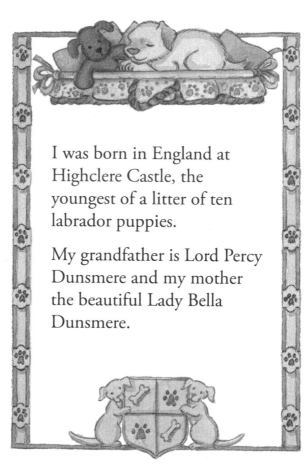

I was born in England at Highclere Castle, the youngest of a litter of ten labrador puppies.

My grandfather is Lord Percy Dunsmere and my mother the beautiful Lady Bella Dunsmere.

We were all given grand Dunsmere names.

Mine is Queen of Snoreway Ninkompoop Finse Daisy Dunsmere. But everyone knows me just as Finse.

I had a wonderful puppyhood with my brothers and sisters. We played all over the castle.

I loved running up and down the stairs in the Great Hall and sliding down the bannisters.

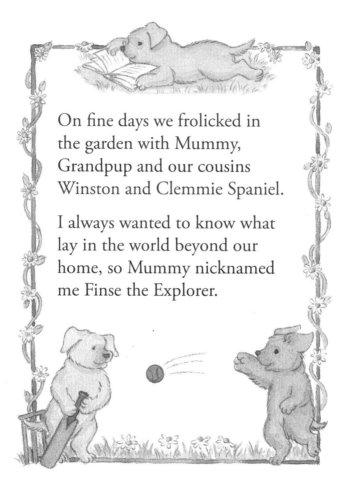

On fine days we frolicked in
the garden with Mummy,
Grandpup and our cousins
Winston and Clemmie Spaniel.

I always wanted to know what
lay in the world beyond our
home, so Mummy nicknamed
me Finse the Explorer.

In wintertime, we played in the snow. I loved sliding down the slopes on my tummy.

I built snowdogs and had snowball fights with my brothers and sisters.

We all gathered together to watch the filming of the television series Dogton Abbey. It was very exciting.

We liked all the actors, though Grandpup was rather jealous of Pharaoh, the handsome star.

When we were older, it was time for us to leave for new homes and kind families who would care for us. Except for my brothers, Alfie and Scoobie, who decided to stay with Mummy and Grandpup at Highclere Castle.

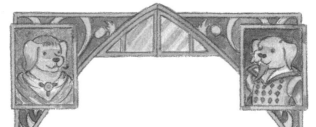

I was the last to leave and took
Fuddlewuddle, my favourite toy.

When I said goodbye to
Mummy and Grandpup, they
gave me a compass so that
I would not get lost.

I was on the way to my
new home.

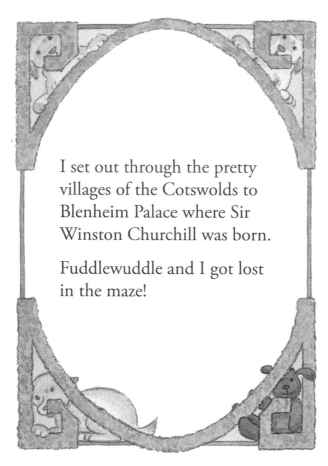

I set out through the pretty villages of the Cotswolds to Blenheim Palace where Sir Winston Churchill was born.

Fuddlewuddle and I got lost in the maze!

Then I visited the great
university town of Oxford
where I saw students riding
bicycles and their professors in
caps and gowns.

I enjoyed looking at the many
beautiful college buildings.

23

I went on to Windsor Castle.
The Queen was there that
day and Her Majesty waved
at everyone.

The guardsmen looked very
handsome in their red coats
and bearskin hats.

At last I arrived in London where I saw Tower Bridge, the Houses of Parliament and Big Ben.

I met Beefeaters at the Tower of London and travellers from all over the world.

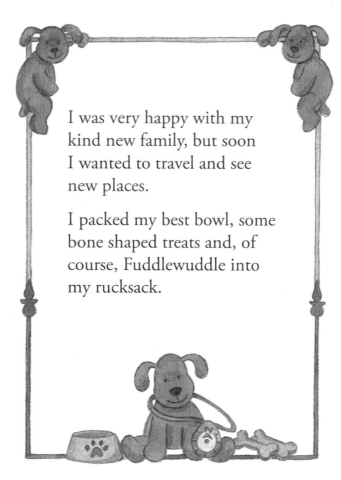

I was very happy with my kind new family, but soon I wanted to travel and see new places.

I packed my best bowl, some bone shaped treats and, of course, Fuddlewuddle into my rucksack.

It was time to start out on
my first great adventure.

I was going to explore the world!

DOGOLOGY

Finse's family are Labradors, but there are many other breeds in the world. Here are some that Finse met in this book: